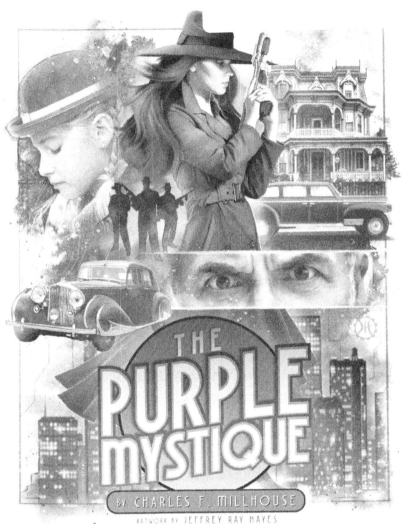

THE PURPLE MYSTIQUE

BY CHARLES F. MILLHOUSE

ARTWORK BY JEFFREY RAY HAYES

I

stormgatepress.com
stormgatepress@gmail.com

First Printing: 2024
ISBN: 9798325333125
Imprint: Independently published

Introducing the Stormgate Press Quick Read Books

Short Story Pulp Adventure Books reminiscent of the dime store novels of old.

BOOK 1: The Purple Mystique

BOOK 2: Night Vision

BOOK 3: A Zane Carrington Adventure

Watch for more books in the series coming soon...

2 A STORMGATE PRESS QUICK READ BOOK

NIGHT VISION

CHARLES F. MILLHOUSE

A NIGHT IN PURPLE

"There isn't corrupt business or legitimate business, there is only business. If I have to crack a few heads to get it done, I've done my business."
Bobby "Two-Tone" Boyce 1939

"You've crippled me...!" Buck Ugerson snarled.

"I should snap your neck for lying to me," the soft voice came from the shadows.

"If... if I tell you what you want to know Two-Tone will hang me out to dry." Ugerson said, his voice less abrasive. He sat tied to a chair in a dark warehouse on the east side of Chicago, his kneecaps shattered – scarlet stained his lips.

"Right now, Bobby Two-Tone is the least of your worries. You should worry about what I'm going to do about you."

A frightened smile broke on Ugerson's lips. "I know your reputation," he said. His voice less than convincing when he added, "But that's all it is, a reputation. You," he swallowed. "You, don't scare me."

"You should be scared Ugh," the woman's voice was razor sharp. "How about I make a phone call right now and tell Two-Tone you're singing like a bird. I'm sure he would..."

"No, God no," Ugerson's face twisted in fear. His eyes screwed tight in his head at the thought of what Two-Tone would do to him.

"Then how about it Ugh? Tell me what I want to know. Where is Senator Miller's daughter? Bobby Two-Tone doesn't need to know the information came from you."

Ugerson clamped his jaw tight.

"He's stalling," a man's voice came out of the dark.

"He's scared," she said.

"I don't think he knows."

Ugerson tried shifting in his chair. "Hey, hey... who's that wit you? I thought we were alone."

"You're right. Maybe he doesn't know," the soft voice replied.

"Use your neutralizer on him," the faceless voice said.

"I don't want to waste a cartridge," she replied. "Besides, he'll tell us what we want to know. Isn't that right Ugh?"

Nervous, his voice shaky, Ugerson said, "You'll never make it in time. The little girl is as good as dead."

Her purple blur came out of the shadows – her face masked by a fedora with an oversized brim. Her lips were turned up into a sinister smile and were as purple as the rest of her attire. She thew a fist, making contact with Ugerson's face, and his head snapped back from the punch.

2

"If that child turns up dead, Ugh, you're going to need a coroner, instead of a doctor."

Ugerson's eyes glistened, and he held his breath as Mystique brazened past him and out of the warehouse. The purple Bentley sat with its engine running when she slipped into the back of the car. "What time is it?" she asked.

"Nine-fifteen,"

"Drive," Mystique said.

The man sitting behind the steering wheel, was Donald "Danny" Brocko, a wide brute of a man with slicked back hair, and a square jaw. He was the Purple Mystique's confidant and the only person that knew who she really was. "You sure it's okay leaving him here?" Danny asked as the car sped out onto the street.

Streetlights caught a glimpse of the Purple Mystique's lovely face. She leaned forward and the glimmer of her dark hair reflected in the light. "Just don't let me forget he's here," she said with a lilt of a smile.

"Are you sure you know what you're doing?" Danny asked.

"What do you mean?" she replied.

"I mean, up until now you've only gone after two-bit thugs. Boyce isn't a thug."

"Boyce is the man I'm after. The man I want, and the reason I'm doing this. I've kept in the shadows too long, Danny. After tonight, organized crime in this city will know of the Purple Mystique. Step on it," she said going silent, watching the passing of the streetlights as they flickered throughout the car. Her heart was heavy, she knew she didn't have a lot of time to save the little girl. The word on the street was grave and if she didn't find her this night, there wouldn't be a reason to save the child.

Betty Miller was seven years old. She'd become the city's little darling, and she appeared at almost as many events as her famous father. Baseball games, horseraces, and cotillions where she was the belle of the ball. It's hard to believe that she was taken from the private school she attended without being seen by anyone.

Senator Miller was chairman of the committee against organized crime, and the deciding vote in a move that would crackdown on Two-Tone and people like him. If the vote wasn't reached by midnight, it would be tabled. Because of little Betty's abduction, Senator Miller was wafting. If the vote failed, there wouldn't be anything anyone could do to stop the underworld from taking over... nothing.

The Bentley drove into the Ever-Glenn district on the south side of Chicago thirty minutes later. The area was filled with blue-collar homes, mostly residents of employees who made a living, cooking, driving, or other scrupulous means of in what was commonly known as the "*family business*". It was a close nit community. Wives went to PTA meetings, children played with one another, while the husbands kept their work affairs hush-hush.

The car came to a stop at the corner of Sycamore Street, and Brushing Lane. A late-night fog hazed the streets. Little pinpricks of light from streetlamps dotted the sidewalk and there wasn't a soul in sight, at least no soul that could be seen.

"Brushing Lane ends in a cul-de-sac, that's where Creedence lives. I don't dare go any further," Danny said as he turned toward Mystique. "I mean we aren't exactly driving a conspicuous car, and I don't want to be caught with no way out."

Mystique took her pistol from its holster inside her jacket. The specially built neutralizer was of her own design and fired a strong mind-altering vapor that rendered an attacker susceptible to suggestion. The chamber atop the weapon was full of the compound she created and swished around inside the glass tube like concentrated smoke. "I'll go alone," she said as she opened the car door.

"Hey, wait. I'm supposed to be your backup."

"You are," she said as she slipped out of the Bentley. "Keep the engine running."

Danny rolled down his car door window and said in a whisper, "I hate when you do this."

"You know our deal," Mystique said. "I have to be seen doing this alone. Are you going to break your promise?"

Danny's face went slack, and he said, "This Catholic boy doesn't go back on his word."

"Good," Mystique said as she closed the back door. "Wait here, I don't know how long I'll be."

The Purple Mystique kept to the shadows. From the moment she left the car she sensed the presence of someone watching her, which made sense. You didn't work for a crime family without making enemies. The prudent thing was to have someone on guard. She blended into the fog, and out of the streetlights passing from tree to shrubs

7

and back to trees again, scrutinizing her every action, watching any possible ways she could be approached.

Whoever Mystique sensed, they were good at hiding, but she figured the best way to bring them out into the open was to give them a reason. She kept on her objective.

Sixty-three Bushing Lane was a large white home at the back of the cul-de-sac and surrounded by a red brick retaining wall was a front for a lovely flower garden, but clearly was a buffer from the street to the house, and a good hiding place for an armed man to hide.

It was clear that Creedence D'Angelo lived in fear. He would be stupid not to. You don't gain the reputation as a clean-up man, not to take precautions. If he had the little girl in the house, then it wouldn't be simple getting in. Mystique paused. The house was dark, but there were several exterior lights illuminating the front walk leading around the side of the home. Her best bet would be to approach the house from the adjoining yard and keep in the dark. When she turned and crossed up a small incline into the grass of the adjacent yard, she heard...

"That's far enough."

The Purple Mystique didn't turn. Keeping her arms loose to her side, she waited for the right opportunity.

"Who's are you?" the man asked in a nasally tone. "What business do you have here?"

Mystique didn't answer. The man might sound unintelligent, but she doubted he was. She closed her eyes and smelled gun oil – he was holding a pistol, a thirty-eight if she was to wager.

"Hey, I'm talking to you."

She sensed her assailant was too far away for her to act, so keeping her voice firm, Mystique said, "Whcre is she... what have you done to her."

"Alright, that's enough," the man said and took a couple steps closer.

Mystique's muscles tightened and she prepared to deliver a roundabout – a firm kick to the face. When she released the stored energy and began her spin, the ground dropped out from under her, and she plummeted into black.

The Purple Mystique hit the ground hard, a sharp wheeze gagged her as she tried to refill her lungs with fresh air. Spots filled her vision, and there was a knife pain slicing up her vertebrae. When she moved up onto the balls of her hands, she fought the urge to cry out. The sudden drop did more than surprise her. It scared the hell out of her. She craned her head upward when the sound of a trap door slammed shut, leaving her in total darkness. She took control of her breath and steadied her nerves.

Danny was right. Up until now she only went after two-bit thugs, easy marks for a fledging vigilante. The people she was after now were prepared for someone like her. Maybe it was because of the NightVision in New York, that the bosses in Chicago were prepared. Or maybe they always lived in fear that someone like her would come for them one day.

From inside the folds of her trench coat she produced a flashlight. The light beam cut through a hazy dense layer of dust filtering on the air, probably due to her impact on the ground.

The Purple Mystique was inside a tunnel, cut through the Earth, and shored up with timber. The crevasse led in one direction, and she slowly navigated her way through it keeping her senses sharp.

She grimaced, the pain from her fall was intense, and more than she had ever endured, but she pushed on, remembering what her grandfather told her: "When you're against the ropes the only thing you can trust in, is yourself, and God."

The Mystique kept her wits about her and said a silent prayer as she pushed on: *Grant me strength and perseverance so that I might find the child and be triumphant this day.*

She followed the path for several minutes in awe of its size and achievement, wondering how much good the people in organized crime could do if they turned their minds to helping instead of hurting.

The ground turned up in a steep incline as she came to a door. She paused studying the unfinished oak and gazed at the doorhandle preparing herself for what was on the other side. She flipped a switch on the side of her weapon, and it clicked into place.

When she took ahold of the handle, the Purple Mystique's body went rigid, and light exploded behind her eyes. An intense wave of power surged throughout her, and she wanted to scream, but couldn't – every joint and muscle in her was locked, thoughts froze in her as her vision blurred, everything became a milky white and then black.

The shock only lasted a few seconds, and when Mystique woke up she found herself lying face down on a thick plush carpet. Her eyes fluttered and adjusted to the dim light in the room. She jerked, realizing her fedora was off her head and her jacket had been removed.

"You're awake," a slippery voice said.

Mystique pushed herself up on her arms.

"I don't know why you hide your face with that hat. It is quite lovely."

Mystique's eyes adjusted to the light. Several feet from her she found Creedence D'Angelo. He wasn't an impressive man, but totally the opposite. He was pudgy, with a dark bowl haircut, and deep reset eyes. A black birthmark, the size of a silver dollar graced his cheek just under his right eye and scorched his Italian heritage. His dark pinstripe suit was tailormade, from C. Wojniak in downtown Chicago.

Her eyes fell on the neutralizer in Creedence's hands as he flaunted it in front of her. *It's been less than ten minutes,* she thought.

"It's very impressive weapon. But didn't your daddy tell you guns weren't for a pretty girl like you?" he said in a deep chauvinistic tone.

Mystique held her reply. She didn't want to play into his mind games. Instead, she pulled herself up on her knees and surveyed the room.

"That's right. we're alone," Creedence said. "You're powerless, especially since I have your weapon. But don't underestimate me," he lifted a forty-four from his lap. "I might not understand your gun, but this one I understand.

So don't do anything funny, or I'll blow a hole clean through you."

Mystique hitched a smile.

"All we have to do is wait here. When the deed is done, Two-Tone will want to talk to you."

Keeping her voice neutral, Mystique said, "Deed?"

"Don't be so daft," Creedence said. "The kid, you know. If daddy does his job and votes against the bill…"

"You'll what?" Mystique said, forcing herself to remain calm. "Let the girl go. We both know that's not going to happen, so don't talk down to me because I'm a woman. That child is as good as dead, and we both know it."

Creedence chuckled, and said, "You aren't some dumb bimbo, are ya? Two-Tone will respect that."

"I don't care what Bobby Two-Tone respects. But if that girl dies, he'll wish to hell he would've never heard of me."

This time Creedence gave a deep throaty laughed that roared up from the pit of his stomach. "This isn't some purse snatcher or mugging you're stopping. This is organized crime, and we are organized. You don't think Ugh gave up my name because he's afraid of you, did you?"

Mystique held her breath and forced a calm glance.

"Two-Tone wanted you here. He wanted me to hold you until we offed that kid. Ugerson did his job because he's afraid of me and Two-Tone. Don't get delusions the underworld is afraid of the Purple Mystique because we aren't."

Mystique's heart throbbed, and the blood coursed through her like a gushing river. The name Bobby "Two-

Tone" Boyce sent ribbons of anger flashing over her eyesight.

"You just sit tight my pretty dove. There's nothing you can do about it now."

The Purple Mystique garnished a fake smile, and said, "You're right."

"Huh?" Creedence's eyebrows raised.

"You aren't two-bit thieves off the street and my actions over the last several months was more of a calling card than idle threats. You might be organized. But I'm organized too, and you shouldn't underestimate *me*."

"Playtime is over little girl," Creedence said. "And..." before he could finish his next sentence, a click came from the neutralizer and Creedence glanced down at it a microsecond before it expelled its beautiful violet mist.

It bloomed, hitting him in the face, shading the air around him in amethyst. Mystique moved to her feet and ambled across the floor. She stopped inches from Creedence and took the forty-four from his hand, unloading the bullets to the carpet and taking her gas gun away from him. "You've inhaled, the purple mystique," she said, altering the tone of her voice into an unusual harmonic. "It is a special strain from the Malva Sylvestris plant in Southeast Asia," she told him. "It will hold you there, partially paralyzed until it leaves your system. Until then you are amenable to the wills of others."

Creedence's eyes were agape, locked in fear, that the Purple Mystique saw many times. "Where is little Betty Miller?" she asked.

Creedence forced himself not to talk. Fighting to keep the words from escaping his lips – gagging on them. "Tell me...!" she yelled.

Strains of water teared down Creedence's face. Fighting harder and harder to hold the words in. The Purple Mystique shoved her stiletto into his chest and pressed hard, screaming, and asking again, "Where is Betty Miller!"

"At... at the pier..." Creedence struggled to keep it in, his eyes bulged from his head. "Sl... sl... slip twenty-nine. She's to be drowned at twelve o'one, regardless of how her father votes."

The Purple Mystique eyed a clock sitting on a table at the other side of the room. *Eleven-twenty-five.* She went for her fedora on the floor, and snagged her coat draped over a chair. Donning her coat, and pulling the hat over her eyes, she said, "You will forget I was ever here. You will tell Two-Tone I never arrived."

"I will tell Two-Tone you never arrived," Creedence said in obedience.

"*And* you will forget what I look like... you forget every detail of my face.

"I will forget every detail of your face."

"Do you understand?"

"I understand," Creedence replied.

Her weapon primed. The Purple Mystique checked the hallway outside the room. The area was clear, but she was wary. Someone outside baited and lured her to the trap door. Cautious, she brazened down the corridor to the top the stairs. Time was not on her side. It would take almost

14

thirty minutes to get to the pier. Thankfully the traffic at night would be light, and Danny would have to break a few traffic laws to make sure they arrived on time.

She navigated down the stairs, scouring the area for anyone. There had to be servants. A maid or butler, even at this late hour. Stopping at the bottom, she paused listening for any movement – the front door was five feet ahead of her. When she reached the door, she hesitated, remembering what happened the last time she went for a handle. She didn't have time to be squeamish, took hold of the doorknob and threw back the door.

Tick

Tock

Tick

Tock... time was not on her side.

Off the front porch the Purple Mystique charged but she only made it five or six paces down the walk when a hard object came to her back.

"Take another step dolly..."

The Purple Mystique didn't have time for games. Lightening quick she wheeled around, bringing her fist along with her. Being taught at a very early age, when you throw a punch use the weight of your entire body. The force of the first punch could be the difference between winning and losing a fight.

The man behind her went to the sidewalk, expelling a silent *ah,* when he fell. The Mystique kicked the man's pistol aside and continued up the walk.

Tick

Tock

Tick

Tock.

"What happened to you?" Danny asked. He stood outside of the Bentley. Several cigarette butts lay around him, and fresh one burned between the fingers of his right hand. "It's been..."

"Twenty minutes," the Purple Mystique said as she climbed into the backseat of the car. "Put that out and get in," she ordered.

Danny slid in behind the steering wheel and brought the engine alive. He shoved the column gear into reverse and raced backward down the street after Mystique told him where to go. He whipped the car into a driveway, slammed the Bentley into first gear and raced down the street.

"You want to tell me what the hell happened back there?"

"Not now... concentrate on the road, Danny. If we are thirty seconds late, little Betty Miller is as good as dead.

Danny glanced at her in the rearview mirror for a split second. He pressed the accelerator to the floor, dragging more and more power of the straight six. He glanced at his watch. "We aren't going..."

"Faster," Mystique interrupted. "You've got to go faster, Danny." She rubbed her hands together, the idea of arriving too late grinded at her. She closed her eyes and set back. The face of Bobby Two-Tone, cut through her like a knife. His hard unwavering eyes, the eyes of a killer were forever burned into her soul. As long as she lived she would never forget them, nor would she forget what the gangster took from her. How he destroyed her life with a simple word. If

16

it was the last thing she would ever do, she would see him brought to his knees, destroyed – everything he ever care for ripped away from him.

The feeling of euphoria encapsulated her at the thought of Two-Tone broken. The car screeched to a stop, tossing the Purple Mystique forward. Her eyes focused as a roaring locomotive charged by the front of the car. Her heart sank.

"Now what?" Danny asked.

Mystique gripped the seat in front of her.

Tick

Tock

Tick

Tock

The chugging tugboat sounded its horn as it crossed the harbor, and little Betty
Miller sat on the dock. Her hands tied behind her back. She watched the boat fade away.

A dense layer of fog rolled its way into the harbor and blanketed the area in a silk curtain. She heard people in the distance, but they were too far away to call for help, and she doubted they would arrive in time anyway.

She fixed her eyes of the murky water, the lights from the city sparkled in the distance looked like little jewels. Her parents were in there somewhere, looking for her. she worked hard to control the water flooding her eyes. She didn't want the two bad men to see her cry.

"Don't worry kid, you'll be out there soon enough."

"Hey, why you have to taunt her like that Frankie?"

Frankie, No Nose, stood on the end of the pier puffing on a short cigar. The smoke lingered around him like a halo. He gained the nickname No Nose after a knife fight went wrong and the end of his nose was sliced off. "What skin is it off your back Charlie?" he asked. "We were told to off the kid. How she feels is irrelevant. We have the easy job. She has to do the dying." He gave a throaty laugh.

Charlie looked down at the kid. "He don't mean noth'n by it kid. Business is business, you know?" Charlie said. He tucked of his jacket and straightened his tie. Killing someone made him nervous, even though he'd done it more times than he could count. It was a ritual of his, to prepare himself. Killing was second nature to him but killing a child – it wasn't something he did every day. That took a special kind of evil, and Charlie Nox, *wasn't* that kind of evil. Even though he knew it needed to be done.

Betty rolled her eyes up at Charlie, but the gag in her mouth prevented her for saying anything. Not that she would. From the time she was snatched at school she barely uttered two words. Scared, and wanting her mommy she didn't understand any of what was happening.

"Hey, I'm cold, tired and need a beer," Frankie said. "Let's do it now and get out of here."

"We still have two minutes," Charlie said. "We wait."

"What's two minutes?"

"Mister Boyce wants to send, what did he call it.. a message. We do it as ordered, twelve o'one and not a second before."

"How's Two-Tone gonna to know?"

"You want to take that risk, go right ahead. But I'm loyal to *Mister Boyce.*"

His words laced with a laugh, Frankie said, "Frightened is more the word I would use."

Charlie turned away, and looked down at Betty, and said with a shrug, "I'm sorry kid, it has to be this way." His voice almost regretful. "Hope you understand." He sharpened his gaze on Betty's eyes. She was glaring at the boardwalk above them. When Charlie followed her stare, he barely had the chance to say, "Holy shit," as he followed the cloaked form through the air as it leapt from the boardwalk – a trail of purple mist in its wake.

Charlie snagged Betty by the scruff of the neck and tossed her over the side of the pier, her little body made a sickly splash when it hit the water.

A second form came off the boardwalk half a second later as it dove into the drink after Betty. Charlie spun around, his pistol out of his shoulder holster, only to be kicked out of his hand – the gun clamored to the wooden planks. He charged forward and the Purple Mystique met him head on, blocking his punch and shoving him backward.

Charlie came in like a boxer, keeping his body low, his fists up in front of his face. The Purple Mystique followed his timing and shifted her footing to match his. She dove to the right, blocked his jab, and threw a punch of her own clipping his jaw. Charlie stumbled back and thumbed his nose. "No dame is going to out fight the Nox," he said. He came in for another pass, but the Purple Mystique didn't have time to play games. She stepped in, cutting Charlie's punch short and blocking his right with her left. Delivering a punch to his stomach, Charlie backed away showing his teeth, Mystique allowed herself a moment and returned his snarl with a smile.

Frankie snagged Mystique in an arm lock from behind. "I got her, Charlie... get her!"

Charlie rush forward his fists up and ready, only he left himself wide open, and the Purple Mystique kicked upward, shoving her foot into his midsection. Charlie bellied over and stumbled back. His form engulfed in the purple haze settling over the pier. He inhaled the smoke, wiping the sting out of his eyes. Then he stopped, his arms dropped to his side, he stood there.

"Charlie?" Frankie questioned. "You okay?"

Charlie didn't reply, he just stood there, catatonic.

"Charlie," The Purple Mystique's voice resonated throughout the dock. "Do my bidding, Charlie. Help me..."

"Hey, what gives?" Franky shrieked as Charlie came out of the amethyst, fists back up. This time however he attacked Frankie, who shoved the Purple Mystique forward as a shield. She rolled to the side, as the two goons threw fists. The pair backed into the lingering purple gas together.

***

The Purple Mystique glanced at the calm water. She staggered forward, prepared to jump in, she ripped off her trench coat and kicked her shoes aside. She turned back to the purple fog as Frankie and Charlie emerged. "Hold," she commanded. Her words echoed on the air.

The two goons stopped, awestruck, their expressions neutral – the whites of their eyes shaded in lavender. "On your knees, and stay there," Mystique ordered, "Do you understand?"

"I understand," both of them said at the same time.

She turned back to the harbor. Her legs coiling tight, ready to jump. Then the black water churned and bubbled, and the head of little Betty Miller broke the surface. Mystique reached for the child and heaved her up to the wooden planks, untying the gag from her mouth, Betty's body heaved and contorted, as she fought to cough the seawater from her lungs. She blinked a few times, and stared into the Purple Mystique's face, trying to see under the shadowed brim. Mystique drew her eyes up to Danny who hauled himself out of the water and dropped to his knees next to them.

"We… we made it," Danny said filling his lungs with fresh air.

"We did," Mystique replied and added, "But let's not cut it that close again."

"Did my mommy and daddy send you?" Betty asked with chattering teeth.

The Purple Mystique regarded the child, and said, "In a way, I guess they did."

"I want to go home," Betty lamented.

The Purple Mystique stood and turned toward the two goons. She eyed the duo, and said, "We will take you home. And then, then we have a message to deliver."

Gunfire erupted from the front lawn of Seventeen Green Forest Road when the Purple Bentley roared to a stop. The bullets ricocheted off of the bulletproof exterior as the backdoor swung open and Frankie and Charlie were expelled onto the sidewalk in front of the luxurious home of Bobby "Two-Tone" Boyce.

The car's engine reeved wickedly as it sat in front of the home. Black smoke poured from the exhaust. The gunfire ceased, and seconds later Two-Tone appeared in the front door of his home, surrounded by dozens of loyal henchmen.

"You think you scare me?" Two-Tone shouted. "You think you frighten me?" He whipped a pistol from inside his coat and unloaded it into the car's driver side window.

The car sat there idling, the dark purple windows impervious to the shrapnel. "You want a war with me...?" Two-Tone asked. "Well, you've got a war... I'm coming for you *Purple Mystique*. There's no place you can hide, no way to protect your identity, and no way to protect your friends, your family from me. By morning there will be a price so large on your head, every hitman from here to Crown City will be gunning for you...!"

The Bentley slowly drove away, as several more gunshots tinged off the exterior. The Purple Mystique sat quietly in the backseat. She glanced up to see Danny staring at her in the rearview mirror.

"You got what you wanted," Danny said. "He knows you exist now."

"Yes, I guess that he does," Mystique replied.

"I don't know why we just didn't drop those two off at the police station instead of letting them go back to Boyce."

"Danny, you know as well as I do, that Charlie and Frankie would be back on the street by daylight. They

22

worked better as a calling card, something for them to tell Two-Tone."

"Yes, I suppose you're right. So, what do we do now?"

"We sit low for a few weeks. Let Two-Tone think that he scared us, and then when he feels safe, we go to work."

"And what if he finds out who you are?"

A devious smile curled up on Mystique's lips. "You're giving Bobby "Two-Tone" Boyce too much credit," she said. "It will be a cold day in hell, before he figures out who I am."

FIN.

CHARLES F. MILLHOUSE

DEATH IN PURPLE

Chicago Tribune headline reads: `Death in Purple Grips City in Panic`... `Killing Spree Leaves Police Baffled.`

Danny Brocko stood in a warehouse off Fleet Street nervously pacing around the parked purple Bentley waiting for the phone to ring. With the police out in force looking for the cause of these strange murders he was sure that he wouldn't get the call. He was sure she wouldn't want to go out tonight.

Even though Danny believed in the Purple Mystique's mission, he worried about her. While it was true that Mystique was highly skilled, incredibly smart, and sufferingly strong willed to the point that it sometimes clouds her judgment, Danny knew her weakness better than anyone.

Bobby 'Two Tone" Boyce was one, that could get her killed. When she approached Danny with the plan to rid Chicago of the underworld boss and get revenge for what he did to her, Danny signed on without compunction. In the year since the Purple Mystique made her first appearance, her enigma grew. While she fought penny ante street thugs to begin with, it wasn't until she went against Boyce that Danny became concerned.

He kept her secret, became her footman, and watched her back. It wasn't until the murders that there was a real risk that Mystique could get caught. Someone, and it went without much speculation as to who, was causing the killings using a deadly form of gas reminiscent of Mystique's own amethyst gas. There were sightings of someone dressed in purple and even a sketched image from an eyewitness that drew the police's attention toward the Purple Mystique.

With tensions high, and with no rhyme or reason for the killings, the people in the city were in a panic. There was no reason for her to go out tonight, yet when the phone rang, Danny picked it up, and did what he signed on to do, be there for her, every time she called.

With the phone receiver clutched in his fist, he said, "Danny here."

"There's been another killing," Mystique's voice was lilt and calm. "The Delaware Building. Meet me on Wabash, at the regular place. I'll be waiting." The phone clicked and went dead.

Twenty minutes later, Danny pulled the Bentley down an alley and parked. Leaving the engine running, he waited. When the car's backdoor opened and closed, he caught the whiff of a local Chinese restaurant and then the image of Mystique in his rearview mirror. He wanted to question her, he wanted to tell her this was a bad idea and that they should stay low until the police caught the killer. Instead, he said dutifully, "Where to?"

Mystique's face was masked in shadow, and even though Danny knew every conure of her face, when she dressed in her purple garb, there was a surreptitious demeanor about her, that even he didn't recognize.

"Randolph Street," she said. "The Delaware Building. When they pulled out of the alley, the streetlights through the windshield caught Mystique's purple lips. There was a seriousness about her, and even though the fedora masked most of her features, Danny could sense her dread.

At ten o'clock there were very few cars on the streets, and a purple Bentley was hard to obscure. The few pedestrians gave the car a curious glance, but Danny kept his speed slow and his course steady.

"Pull over here," Mystique said.

Bringing the car to a stop along the curb several blocks from the Delaware house, Danny turned around in his seat and regarded Mystique. "Now what?" he asked.

"The police have the building surrounded," Mystique said. "Evidently, they have a suspect cornered but they've yet to move in."

"You realize this is a trap," Danny said bluntly.

Since the death of the police commissioner last year Bobby "Two Tone" Boyce controlled a large portion of the police department. What good cops there were, were unable to fight the injustices going on within the city's government. With the mayor and the new commissioner in his back pocket, Boyce had little to fear, and he has run amuck since.

Without a doubt the purple murders were his doing, and a surefire way of capturing the Purple Mystique.

"I'm going in there," Mystique said.

A wash of anxiety chilled Danny's body. "This is a big gamble," he said. "For over a year you've stayed and worked in the shadows. If you do this, there will be no turning back."

"I can't keep hidden any longer," Mystique said sharply. "If I'm to take the fight to Boyce. Organized crime knows of my existence. Now it's time for the city to know what I stand for. Boyce become so powerful, that not even the governor dares to go up against him."

"Did it ever dawn on you that the Feds can handle this?" Danny asked.

Mystique's lips formed into a hard little line, and her voice was heavy when she spoke. "It wasn't the Feds whose lives were destroyed by Bobby Boyce.," she explained. It wasn't their world destroyed by his murderous ways. It wasn't..." she swallowed and bit off her last word.

Danny wanted to tell her he was sorry, but Mystique would regard that as sympathy, and she had little time for that. Instead, he asked, "What's the plan?"

"Give me fifteen minutes, park the car and go to the building. Do you have your reporter credentials with you?"

"Of course," Danny replied touching the shirt pocket under his jacket.

"Then go make some noise, ask a lot of questions," Mystique said. "There will be a lot of onlookers, even at this time of night. Time to stir the pot a little. You understand."

Danny replied with a sharp nod, and without another word, the Purple Mystique slipped out of the Bentley and disappeared into the shadows of a close by side street.

As instructed, Danny parked the car in a secluded parking lot, and with fedora on his head, and with his press credentials safely tucked into the brim of his hat, he made his way toward the Delaware Building. Police spotlights crisscrossed beams of light over the building, scouring every inch of the structure.

As Mystique predicted the block was cordoned off with police officers and an ever-growing group of spectators. Muscling his way through the crowd exclaiming, "Press here, press here. Make way for the press." Danny worked his way to the barricade half a block away from the building.

A plain clothed officer was fielding questions, and it didn't take Danny long to bring attention to himself when he asked, "Is she in there... this Purple Mystique we've been hearing about?"

With a disgruntled look on his thin face, the officer said, "There is no Purple Mystique. Whoever this woman is, she's a killer."

"But didn't she rescue Senator Miller's daughter last month?" Why would she turn to murder if she saved a little girl's life."

"Who are you?" the officer asked.

"Danny Brocko of the Chicago Defender," he replied.

"Well, Mr. Brocko, I don't know where you get your information, or your sources, but there is no evidence of a Purple Mystique terrorizing the local members of organized crime."

"I didn't say she was," Danny said. "I merely pointed out that she saved a little girl's life. As far as I know there wasn't any members of organized crime involved with that kidnapping, or are there?"

"Is there any truth to your statement, is there a link to the Miller case and Bobby "Two Tone" Boyce?" another reporter asked.

A third second reporter spoke up, and asked, "Can you tell us if Mr. Boyce has been investigated concerning the Miller case?"

"That's all the questions for now," the plainclothes officer said with a sour expression.

"One, more, one more question if I could," Danny said. "For my article, could you give me your name please?"

Hesitant, the officer straightened his tie and said with a clear tone, "Lieutenant William Hatch."

When Danny replied, "Thanks Bill," he received a callous stare from Hatch who turned away as other reporters shouted more questions. When gunfire came from inside the building, gasps filled the gathering. All eyes went to the fifth floor of the high rise and Danny used the distraction to sprint up the street. He did all he could to stir public doubt toward Bobby "Two Tone", now he needed to get inside the building. The Purple Mystique didn't tell him to stay outside, and if anything, it was his job to watch her back.

With more gunfire coming from the fifth floor, Danny didn't have any trouble breaking through the police line and entering the building from the south entrance. Entering undetected, he thought he had made it scot-free, until he heard, "Hey, you there, *STOP.*"

Smashing his way through the door of the stairway, he ran up, skipping steps as he went. Having played football in college, Danny had the physical physique to rush ahead without becoming winded.

When Danny entered the fifth floor the entire level was engulfed in purple mist. Not having an immunity for the amethyst gas, the same as Mystique, be placed a small breathing apparatus over his nose and mouth and took a deep breath.

Shadows were everywhere. The only light on the floor came from the massive spotlights outside beaming powerful light through the windows. Danny went cautiously forward. The level was partitioned off into offices with one centralized corridor running between them. When the form of the Purple Mystique passed into the hallway from one doorway, crossing the hall into another, Danny rushed ahead. She was on the prowl, which meant whoever was up here, she was close to finding them.

He followed Mystique into the room, hoping to assist her. Eerily dark, he quickly noticed a connecting door to the adjoining office, and Mystique stood in the center of the room staring in its direction.

Making his presence known, he said, "Hey, it's me." He reached out for her, but when he laid his hand on her shoulder, all he found was muscle.

When the form turned, the bristly face of a man in drag took Danny by surprise. "Holy hell!" he exclaimed as the doppelganger took a swing at him. Avoiding the punch by diving under it, he came back up, fist at the ready clobbering the man across the chin, knocking the fake Mystique backward.

As the phony recovered, he raised a pistol. Danny dove behind a darkened desk as the man opened fire. Splinters of wood flung into the air, chipping away at the desk.

Reaching into his jacket for the 9mm at his side, Danny pushed over the desk, raised up to fire, but the fake Mystique was gone. He quickly turned his gun towards the inner door of the room and drew a breath, *I'll be damned,* he chagrinned. As he regained his footing, a handful of uniformed police officers stormed the room, their weapons raised they shouted, "Don't move–"

"Drop your weapon–"

"Get your hands up–"

Before Danny could react, the Purple Mystique came into the room behind the officers with her amethyst gun out in front of her. The light from outside caught the curvature of her body, and it was undoubtedly the real deal.

When her weapon discharged, it made a *foom whoop* sound, discharging a pellet filled with her neuro paralyzing drug. The police officers were encompassed inside her noxious vapor. They didn't have time to react, before the gas disabled them. They stood motionless; their eyes glazed in violet.

"Your timing is impeccable," Danny said joining Mystique.

"There's still a killer in here," Mystique replied. "Don't let your guard down."

"How did your fake manage to overcome your gas?" Danny asked.

"Simple, it isn't mine. Like my doppelganger, it's fake. I've only just now fired my weapon."

"But news reports claim the murders were done by using a poisonous gas, we assumed they had mimicked your amethyst gas."

"Fake information fed to the press," mystique said.

"And the murder victim?"

Mystique hooked a thumb over her shoulder, and said, "Through there. The victim is a man in his late forties. A family man by the photographs on the wall."

"And they killed him to do what?"

"Let's find out," Mystique said facing one of the paralyzed officers. "I'm going to ask you some questions," she began. Her voice was calm and alluring. "Who gave you your orders?"

Without hesitation, the officer replied, "Lieutenant Hatch."

"And what were those orders?" she asked.

"Secure this floor," the officer said forcing out his answers. "Trap you, bring you out in handcuffs for the whole city to see."

Mystique glanced at Danny, and then back to the officer. "You might get that chance," she said.

"Lookout...!" Danny shouted as the fake Mystique burst into the room. He and the Purple Mystique dove for cover as the fake opened fire; his wild shots filled the room striking windows, walls, furniture, pictures and even one of the succumbed police officers – sending the man to the floor in a pool of blood. In less than a minute the fake Mystique disappeared and only the echo of his weapon remained.

"What the hell was that all about?"

"Our impersonator must have orders not to kill me, but to capture me," Mystique said. "To discredit me, they must have me alive."

"So, we have an advantage," Danny said receiving a curious look from the Purple Mystique. "Well since he can't kill you..."

"Man is like an animal," Mystique said. "If you corner him, he will do whatever he has to, to survive."

"What's our next move, then?"

"You being here has put a spanner in his plan," Mystique said. "He'll be gunning for you, so..."

"I'm bate?"

"You came up here," Mystique said, with a little lift to the corner of her mouth.

"When am I going to learn to stay out of the way?"

"I don't think that's ever going to happen," Mystique replied with a smile in her words. "We have to hurry. If these officers don't take me out in cuffs soon, they'll send more in to find out what's going on."

"Let's get this over with then," Danny said in a less than an enthusiastic tone.

The spotlights from outside continued to pour light in through the windows, catching the fading purple mist as Danny moved out into the corridor between offices. To say he wasn't nervous would be an understatement. It's not like he hadn't come under threat before, only that thought didn't calm his nerves any.

Things were heating up quicker than he expected, though Danny always knew in the back of his mind that the Purple Mystique would change her tactics and begin to oust Bobby Boyce. Her entire plan was to get under Two Tone's skin, and even after thwarting his attempt to corrupt Senator Miller, it didn't take the gangster long to come after her.

This murder spree is just Boyce's first attempt. It was a fair bet to say that he wouldn't stop after this. If anything, he'll do whatever he can to find the Purple Mystique's true identity. *That's going to be a shocker,* Danny thought.

When movement came from up ahead, Danny cleared his thoughts, and narrowed his resolve. He drew up his pistol, aimed down the barrel of the revolver and took slow steady steps forward.

At that moment, the form of the Purple Mystique came into the corridor. Danny hesitated. Through the darkness, he couldn't tell if it was the real Mystique, or the fake. His gun arm shook, his finger rested against the trigger, and he held his breath unsure of what to do.

As a sharp sting bit into his shoulder, Danny realized who he was facing, but it was too late. He winced, stumbled back, barely on his feet, his head swimming he tried to focus.

Fighting the pain, he was unable to raise his gun. Through glazed blurry eyes, Danny focused on the fake Mystique, waiting for the fatal shot, but when he heard, *foom whoop,* and saw the gas plume in front of the copycat he allowed himself to relax.

"I've got you," the Purple Mystique said as she took Danny in her arms. "It's over now."

Together they walked toward the fake Mystique who succumbed to the amethyst gas. "Who are you?" the Purple Mystique asked the impersonator.

"Coraven, Nathan Coraven," he said in a hallucinate state.

"Who do you work for?"

"Bobby Boyce," he replied without reservation.

"Well, Mr. Coraven," the Purple Mystique said. "There is something I want you to do for me. Listen very carefully."

Camera flashes exploded outside the Delaware Building, when Nathan Coraven came out of the building escorted by the Chicago police officers. "I did it, I did it...!" he exclaimed.

The reporters forced themselves forward, lunging closer in an attempt to hear the confession. "What do you mean you did it?" one of the reporters shouted.

"I pretended to be the Purple Mystique, to frame her for the murders I committed."

"That's enough talking, now." Lieutenant Hatch said trying to get the reporters to focus on him.

"I was hired by Bobby "Two Tone" Boyce to frame her and turn public opinion against her.

"I thought you said there was no Purple Mystique," a reporter shouted.

Hatch put up his hands as if trying to calm the frenzied reporters. "I assure you there is no Purple Mystique," he said with certainty. "Our perpetrator is suffering from a mental breakdown. I can assure you, the Purple Mystique is a fable, created to dupe the good citizens of Chicago."

"Well, if she doesn't exist," another reporter shouted and pointed to the front of the building. "Who is that?"

More flashbulbs exploded, all eyes went to the front of the Delaware Building to find the flowing trench coat, of a blond-haired woman standing atop the portico overhang. Though her face was shadowed by the oversized fedora, there was no mistaking who she was.

"I want to put the police, the government and Bobby "Two Tone" Boyce on notice," the Purple Mystique said in an amplified tone. "Your corruption is coming to an end. You are no longer safe. Everywhere you turn I will be there. Every face you see, every stranger you meet, be warned it could be me, and when you least expect it, I'll strike."

"Just don't stand there," Hatch ordered. "Get her…!"

Amethyst gas exploded around the Purple Mystique, and before the police officers could rush toward her, she was gone.

Lieutenant Hatch rushed forward, stunned that the Purple Mystique could so easily disappear. "Set up roadblocks within ten blocks from here!" he shouted. "She doesn't get away… do you hear me, she doesn't get away." He turned toward the reporters who stood like wild animals ready to leap onto him with their insipid questions. He swallowed hard, grabbed Coraven by the scruff of the neck pushing him through the crowd to the waiting police car.

Mystique helped Danny into the back of the purple Bentley. "Are you alright?" she asked pulling the fedora from her head.

Danny let out a hesitant breath, and said, "I've been better. But I'm alright."

Mystique slipped into the front seat and brought the car engine alive. "We should get you taken care of," she said.

"Can you get us back to the warehouse?" Danny asked.

"I do know how to drive a car," she replied.

"Sometimes I wonder. I mean you don't have much cause to."

"Very funny," Mystique replied looking at him through the rearview mirror.

Danny blew out another painful breath, and said in a serious tone, "You're in it deep now."

"We knew this was coming," Mystique replied as she pulled the car out onto the road. "But to be honest I would have hoped it would have been more on my terms."

"Bobby Boyce likes to play by his own rules," Danny said. "We can't let him dictate our every move."

"We aren't. Boyce won't see the next move coming," Mystique said.

"He better not," Danny said. "Otherwise, it could be fatal for us."

"I've spent the last several years preparing for this war, Danny. It's a war I intend on winning."

Danny allowed himself to sink further into the oversized backseat. His breath staggered, he winced from the pain in his shoulder. There would be time to worry about that later, he considered. Yet in the back of his mind, he had a funny feeling that soon, there would be no place safe. When next they confronted Bobby Boyce and his people, it would be on her terms.

The Purple Mystique's next plan was daring, bold and a bit insane. For it to work, she would have to be prepared to face him without a disguise, look him in the eye and pretend that she didn't hate his guts.

FIN-

Who is the *mysterious* Purple Mystique…?

What is her connection to Bobby "Two-Tone" Boyce…?

Why is she obsessed with destroying his criminal empire…?

Watch for more action-packed stories of the *Purple Mystique*… COMING SOON!

CHARLES F. MILLHOUSE

ABOUT THE AUTHOR

Charles F. Millhouse is an Award-Winning Author and Publisher. He published his first book in 1999 and he hasn't looked back. Having written over thirty books in the Pulp/Science Fiction genres. His imagination is boundless. From the 1930's adventures of Captain Hawklin – through the gritty paranormal old west town of New Kingdom – to the far-off future in the Origin Trilogy, Charles breathes life into his characters, brings worlds alive and sends his readers on journeys they won't soon forget.

Charles lives in Southeastern, Ohio with his wife and two sons.

Visit stormgatepress.com for more details.